C00 647 354

D0248264

DUNDEE CITY COUNCIL *Space*

CENTRAL LIBRARY

SCHOOL LIBRARY SERVICE

Dundee City Council
Leisure & Communities
CHANGING FOR THE FUTURE

Wendy Smith

A & C Black • London

Rockets series:

CROOK CATCHERS - Karen Wallace & Judy Brown

HAUNTED MOUSE - Dee Shulman

LITTLE T - Frank Rodgers

MOTLEY'S CREW - Margaret Ryan &
Margaret Chamberlain

MR CROC - Frank Rodgers

MRS MAGIC - Wendy Smith

MY FUNNY FAMILY - Colin West

ROVER - Chris Powling & Scoular Anderson

SILLY SAUSAGE - Michaela Morgan & Dee Shulman

SPACE TWINS - Wendy Smith

WIZARD'S BOY - Scoular Anderson

First paperback edition 2003
First published 2002 by A & C Black Publishers Ltd
37 Soho Square, London W1D 3QZ
www.acblack.com

Text and illustrations copyright © 2002 Wendy Smith

The right of Wendy Smith to be identified as author
and illustrator of this work has been asserted by her
in accordance with the Copyright, Designs and Patents Act 1988.

ISBN 0-7136-6110-0

A CIP catalogue record for this book is available
from the British Library.

All rights reserved. No part of this publication may
be reproduced in any form or by any means - graphic,
electronic or mechanical, including photocopying,
recording, taping or information storage and retrieval
systems - without the prior permission in writing of
the publishers.

A & C Black uses paper produced with elemental
chlorine-free pulp, harvested from managed sustainable forests.

Printed and bound by G. Z. Printek, Bilbao, Spain.

Chapter One

Beyond a trillion stars where there is nothing but nothing, the good ship Zazaza zooms across the sky.

Each night it sends a signal.

In the galactaglobe sit the space twins, Mik and Mak. They are about to contact Earth.

LEISURE AND CULTURE DUNDEE	
C00647354X	
Bertrams	21/09/2011
	£4.99
SLS	O\6

Here on Earth, some mega years later, Wilbur Day's glasses twinkle up from East Volesey*.

*a suburb on the fringe of nowhere.

Wilbur and his East Volesey Space Spotter Squad like to speak to their space friends whenever they can.

Wilbur went on.

The raffle was for the East Volesey Football Club. The team needed a new strip.

Mik and Mak agreed to see what they could come up with.

They went to ask Captain Lupo and Zuna, the Dream Supervisor. Fortunately, Captain Lupo was in a good mood.

Chapter Two

Wilbur and his squad were enormously successful in selling their raffle tickets.

A large crowd gathered to see who'd won the special prize. No one thought it would be a *real* trip into space!

Everyone cheered madly as Xavier Price and his mum went to collect the prize.

When they got home Xavier tore open
the envelope.

Xavier and his mum packed their bags
ready to be picked up at 10 p.m.

But Xavier and his mum were not
picked up in the way they expected.

From the spaceship Mik and Mak put
them into a trance and floated them up
to the Zazaza.

When they arrived, they didn't know
where they were.

16

Chapter Three

The next morning Xavier and his mum were looking forward to breakfast.

17

Mrs Price was very keen to get a tan.

19

Mik and Mak loved the idea of playing football.

Xavier helped Mik and Mak make their own football kit.

The three boys played space football.
This was fun at first since the ball
was always jumping up to the ceiling.
And without any gravity boots, Xavier
could float along too.

Xavier had never scored so many goals in his life.

But he scored one too many when he smashed Captain Lupo's prize trophy.

Captain Lupo was in a real rage.

Xavier's mum was even more annoyed.

Chapter Four

It was very clear that Xavier's mum wasn't happy on the good ship Zazaza. And she wasn't the only one.

Captain Lupo wasn't happy either.

Zuna did her best to cheer up Mrs Price.

Mik and Mak signalled to Earth for advice.

Captain Lupo agreed.

He pressed the 'Return' button.

Chapter Five

The Zazaza sped to earth on full power. It hovered over Grafton Parade where the Prices lived.

The street was surprisingly empty.

In a violent flash of green light,
Mrs Price and Xavier were beamed
into their beds and a deep sleep.

At that very moment, Wilbur's mum was hurrying out of the fish and chip shop.

It's not every day you see a flying saucer.
Wilbur's mum went home in a daze.

Of course, nobody believed her.

And nobody was going to believe
Xavier and his mum either. They weren't
quite sure where they'd been themselves.

So they didn't say much.

Wilbur and the squad, of course, did know the truth. So did everyone on board the Zazaza.

Chapter Six

Meanwhile, the raffle had raised a lot of money for the East Volesey Football Club. There was enough to get new strip for the team.

We're having another competition. The winning design will be used for the new strip.

Great.

Wilbur and his friends started designing madly.

But the funkiest design of all came from Xavier Price.

This is how it looked.

glittering
stars on
dark blue
background

a selection
of planets

A gala match was planned to show off
the new outfits. Wilbur told Mik and
Mak all about it.

There was a massive turnout at the East Volesey Football Club.

Under the floodlight the stars dazzled the spectators and the goalie.

The raffle organisers and Xavier watched from the Director's box.

East Volesey won by a spectacular fourteen goals to four.

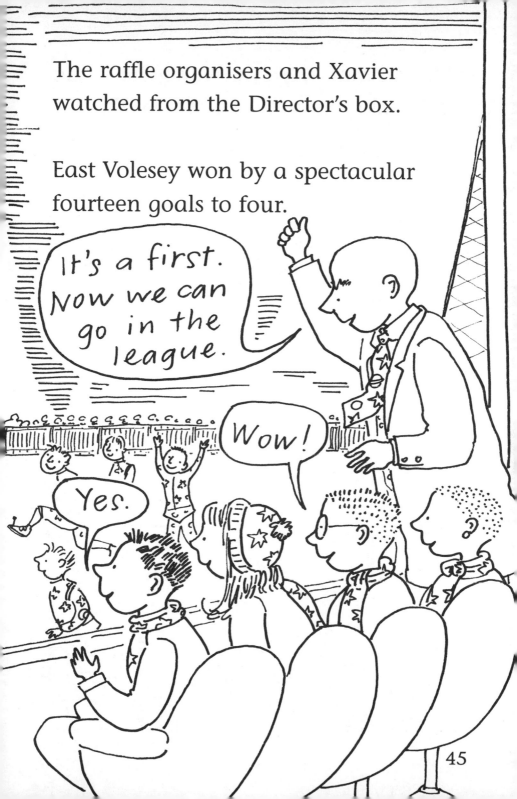

It's a first. Now we can go in the league.

Wow!

Yes.

Mik and Mak were watching the game on the Wundascope. They were thrilled.

Wilbur invited Xavier to become an honorary member of the Space Spotter Squad. Xavier was pleased to have some new friends.

Wilbur assured him they were.

And soon Xavier was friends with Mik and Mak, who each night send a signal.